imals Eat WHAT?!

BLOOD and GUTS

Holly Duhig

Lerner Publications ◆ Minneapolis

First American edition published in 2020 by Lerner Publishing Group, Inc.

Editor: Emilie Dufresne
Design: Jasmine Porter

Lerner Publications Company
An imprint of Lerner Publishing Group, Inc.
241 First Avenue North
Minneapolis, MN 55401 USA

For reading levels and more information, look up this title at www.lernerbooks.com.

Main body text set in VAG Rounded Std. Typeface provided by Adobe Systems.

Photo credits:
Images are courtesy of Shutterstock.com, with thanks to Getty Images, Thinkstock Photo, and iStockphoto. Frederik the Fly: Natthapon Boochagorn & Roi and Roi. Front cover: Sunflowerr, Memo Angeles, MaryValery, Creative Mood, Macrovector, Useless_Graphic, Maquiladora. 5: Eric Isselee, Nathapol Kongseang, LiskaM, photolinc, StockSmartStart, PiXXart. 6: Top Vector Studio, jenykorney. 7: pathdoc, Anastasiia Kucherenko. 8: Paul Reeves Photography. 9: Atovot. 10: MartinMaritz. 11: Jan Mastnik. 12: Karel Cerny. 13: pikepicture. 14: Tao Jiang. 15: Eric Isselee. 16: Iconic Bestiary, Javier Brosch. 18: Cheryl E. Davis. 19: Sara Robinson. 20: Kirill Dorofeev. 21: COMMON THINGS. 22: StudioSmart. 23: Macrovector, Daniel Prudek.

Library of Congress Cataloging-in-Publication Data

Names: Duhig, Holly, author.
Title: Blood and guts / Holly Duhig.
Description: Minneapolis : Lerner Publications, 2020. | Series: Animals eat what? | Includes index. | Audience: Ages 6–10 | Audience: Grades 2–3 | Summary: "Do animals really eat blood and guts? They sure do! Full-color photography and funny facts will engage young readers in learning about the biological processes of living things"— Provided by publisher.
Identifiers: LCCN 2019028062 (print) | LCCN 2019028063 (ebook) | ISBN 9781541579316 (library binding) | ISBN 9781541587038 (paperback) | ISBN 9781541582576 (ebook)
Subjects: LCSH: Bloodsucking animals—Juvenile literature. | Animals—Food—Juvenile literature.
Classification: LCC QL756.55 .D84 2020 (print) | LCC QL756.55 (ebook) | DDC 591.5/3—dc23

LC record available at https://lccn.loc.gov/2019028062
LC ebook record available at https://lccn.loc.gov/2019028063

Manufactured in the United States of America
1-47213-47918-7/16/2019

Contents

Animals Eat What?!   4

Bags of Blood   6

Vampire Bats   8

Biting Bugs   10

Suckers for Blood   12

The Vampire Finch   14

The Kiss of Death   16

Gut Gobblers   18

Intestine Invader   20

Do You Eat Blood and Guts?   22

Glossary   24

Index   24

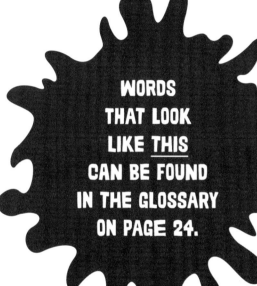

WORDS THAT LOOK LIKE THIS CAN BE FOUND IN THE GLOSSARY ON PAGE 24.

Animals Eat what?!

All animals need to eat food to stay alive. However, some animals have different ideas about what counts as "food."

IT IS I, FREDDY THE FLY, WORLD-FAMOUS CRITIC OF UNUSUAL FOOD!

Bags of Blood

Unless you're a vampire, it has probably never crossed your mind to drink blood. However, for some animals, blood is full of <u>nutrients</u> they need to stay healthy.

Many animals feed on blood, including insects, <u>mammals</u>, fish, and birds! You probably think that drinking blood is gross. This is because, for humans, drinking blood can spread diseases.

NEVER DRINK BLOOD! YOU ARE NOT A VAMPIRE!

Vampire Bats

WATCH OUT! HUMAN BLOOD IS MY FAVORITE!

These blood-sucking critters need no introduction. They are the only known mammals that drink blood as their main source of nutrients. Just like vampires, they use two sharp teeth to bite through their victim's skin.

Vampire bats mainly feed on mammals. They don't let a bit of fur get in their way. The bats have sharp teeth that shave away the fur around the part of the animal they are biting.

THIS IS ALL A BIT MUCH. I FEEL DIZZY!

LOOK:

1

TASTE:

1

SMELL:

1

FEEL:

9

TOTAL SCORE: 12

Biting Bugs

Have you ever found itchy spots on your skin after being outside? If so, you have probably been a mosquito's dinner. Mosquitos "bite" using a proboscis (pro-BOSS-kiss) which they use to suck up blood.

Mosquito saliva (spit) numbs the skin. This makes you less likely to feel the bite and swat the mosquito away. Unfortunately, deadly diseases, such as malaria, can be passed from one human to another in mosquito saliva.

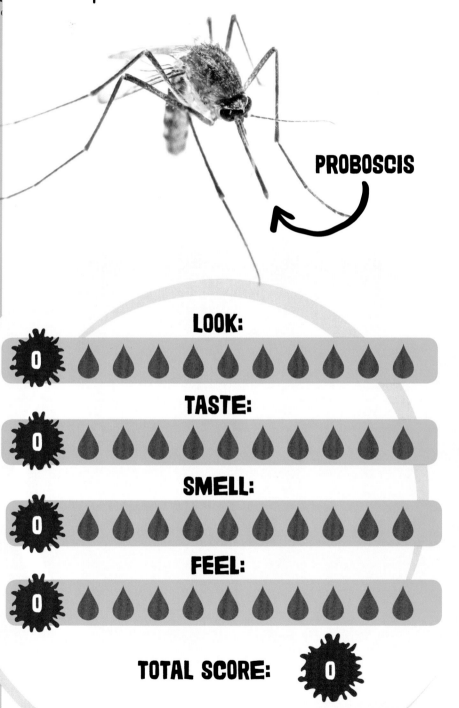

PROBOSCIS

LOOK:

0

TASTE:

0

SMELL:

0

FEEL:

0

TOTAL SCORE: 0

THIS LOOKS DISEASED. I THINK I'LL PASS.

Human Blood

Suckers for Blood

SOME DOCTORS STILL USE LEECHES, BUT ONLY TO IMPROVE BLOOD FLOW.

Some leeches feed on the blood of animals, including humans. In the 19th century, doctors used leeches to remove blood. They thought doing this could cure diseases.

The type of leech used by doctors has three jaws, each with around one hundred sharp teeth! Because of this, the marks they leave on a person's skin are Y-shaped.

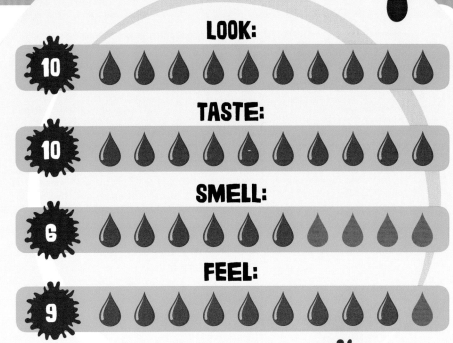

LOOK: 10

TASTE: 10

SMELL: 6

FEEL: 9

TOTAL SCORE: 35

I'M TASTING METAL, IRON, AND NO DISEASES!

The Vampire Finch

BLUE-FOOTED BOOBY

VAMPIRE FINCH

Can you guess what the vampire finch's favorite meal is? That's right, blood! The vampire finch is a bird that lives on the Galápagos Islands. It uses its sharp beak to drink the blood of another bird called the blue-footed booby.

It is thought that the vampire finch didn't always drink blood but started by pecking insects from the booby's feathers. When they pecked too hard, they started drinking the booby's blood too.

NOW THE VAMPIRE FINCH IS CONSIDERED A PARASITE!

HMM, NOT REALLY MY CUP OF TEA. WAIT! IS THERE SOMETHING FLOATING IN THIS? THERE IS. IT'S A BUG!

LOOK:
0

TASTE:
3

SMELL:
3

FEEL:
2

TOTAL SCORE: 8

The Kiss of Death

WANT A KISS?

LAMPREY MOUTHS HAVE ROWS AND ROWS OF TEETH!

Lampreys are long, eel-like fish with a face only a mother could love. Their mouths are like suckers. They attach themselves to other fish and feed on their blood.

Lampreys can stay attached to one fish for weeks. Their mouths act like vacuum cleaners, sucking up as much blood as they can. Some big fish can survive being attacked by a lamprey, but smaller fish usually die from blood loss.

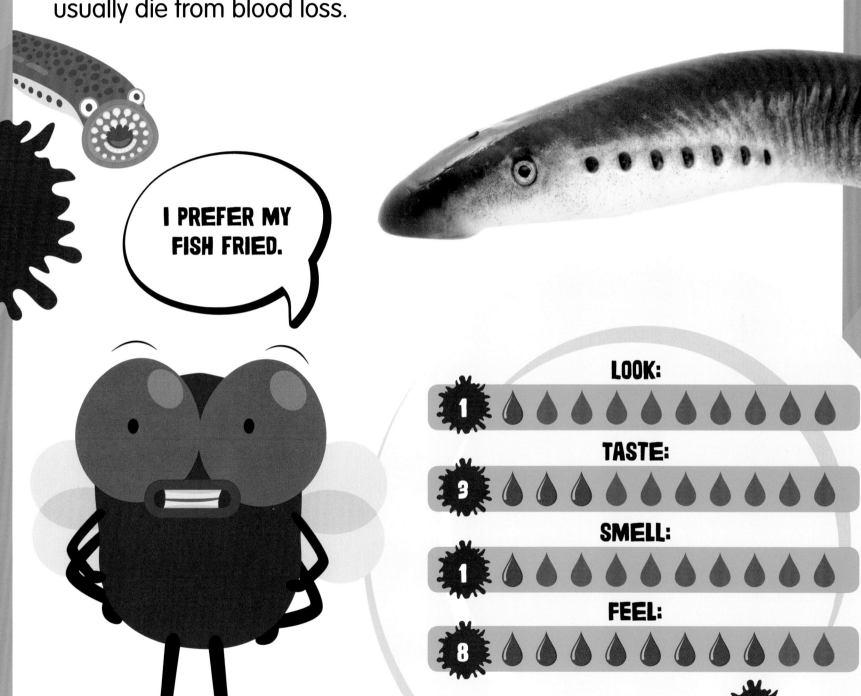

I PREFER MY FISH FRIED.

LOOK: 1

TASTE: 9

SMELL: 1

FEEL: 8

TOTAL SCORE: 19

Gut Gobblers

DO YOU HAVE THE GUTS TO TRY SOME?

When a gray wolf kills its <u>prey</u>, what do you think is the first part of the animal it digs into? The legs? The muscles? The bones? It's none of these. Gray wolves are known for eating the guts of the prey first.

Wolves will usually eat the <u>organs</u> before anything else because they are high in nutrients. Often, wolves will eat the organs of an animal and come back for the rest when they are hungry again.

YOU'LL OFTEN FIND ME BUZZING AROUND A BODY AFTER THE WOLVES HAVE HAD THEIR SHARE. I JUST CAN'T HELP MYSELF.

LOOK:
8

TASTE:
10

SMELL:
9

FEEL:
10

TOTAL SCORE: 37

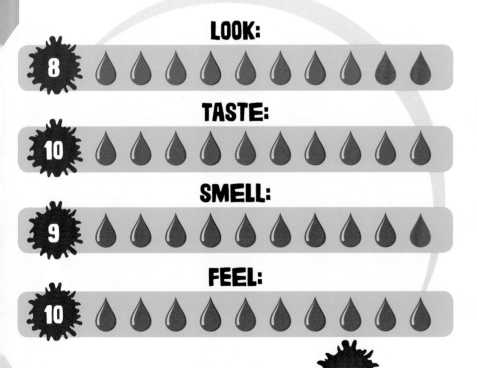

Intestine Invader

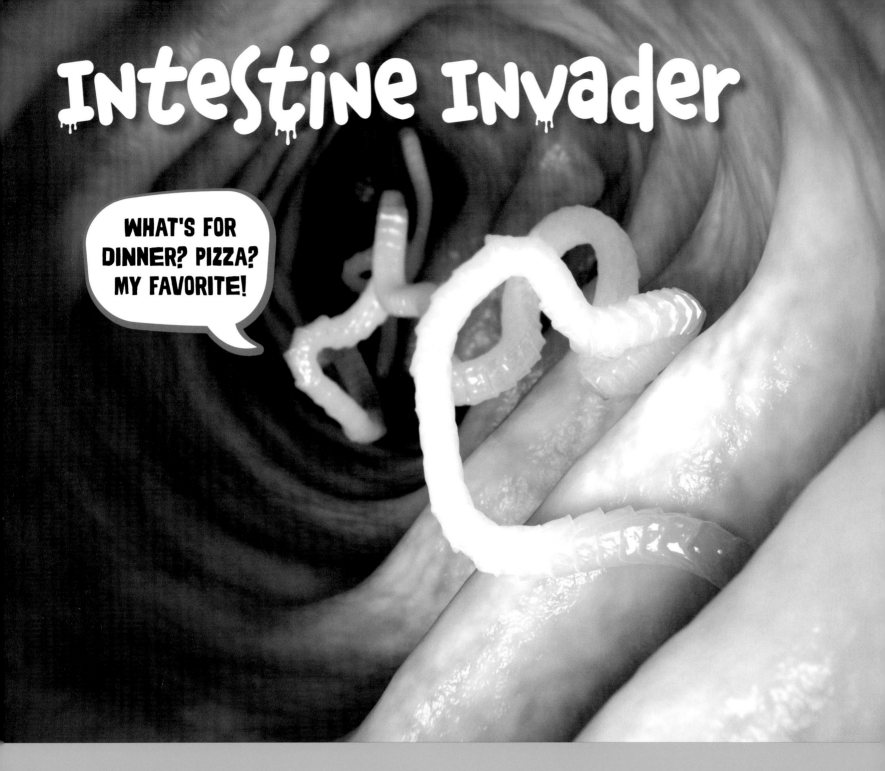

WHAT'S FOR DINNER? PIZZA? MY FAVORITE!

Ever heard of an animal that can eat you from the inside out? No? Well, a tapeworm can! Tapeworms are parasites, which means they survive by stealing nutrients from other living things.

I NEED A NEW JOB. THIS IS TOO MUCH.

Tapeworms can get into your body when you eat something with tapeworm eggs in it. The worm grows inside your <u>intestines</u> and eats the food that you eat. This means your body misses out on those nutrients. You can get very sick if you have tapeworms.

LOOK:

TASTE:

SMELL:

FEEL:

TOTAL SCORE:

Do You Eat Blood and Guts?

BLACK PUDDING IS A SAUSAGE-LIKE FOOD THAT IS MADE FROM PIG'S BLOOD.

Humans usually cook their food before eating it. They do eat blood and guts, though! People eat all sorts of animal organs including hearts, livers, and stomachs.

Haggis is a Scottish food. It is a sheep's stomach stuffed with chopped-up sheep's heart, liver, and lungs.

HAGGIS

FINALLY, SOME REAL SCOTTISH CUISINE.

LOOK:
10

TASTE:
10

SMELL:
10

FEEL:
10

TOTAL SCORE: 40

23

Glossary

CRITIC someone whose job it is to judge something, such as food

CUISINE a type of food related to a particular place

INTESTINES long, coiled tubes below the stomach that help to digest food

MAMMALS animals that have warm blood, a backbone, and produce milk

NUTRIENTS things that plants and animals need to grow and stay healthy

ORGANS parts of the body that have their own specific jobs or functions

PARASITES a plant, animal, or fungus that lives on or in another living thing

PREY animals that are hunted by other animals for food

Index

BITES 8, 10–11

DISEASES 7, 11–13

FISH 7, 16–17

GALÁPAGOS ISLANDS 14

LIVER 22–23

NUTRIENTS 6, 8, 19–21

ORGANS 19, 22

PARASITES 15, 20

PROBOSCIS 10–11

SUCKERS 12, 16

TEETH 8–9, 13, 16

VAMPIRES 6–9, 14–15